unimpressive   Sheri Dixon

I0538747

unimpressive

the inelegant art of

just getting by

By Sheri Dixon

I dedicate this story to the rest of us

No flash, no money

No arsenal, no time

All heart, all grit

All bullheaded determination

Not enough sense to know

That we're not supposed to survive

Much less thrive

But we'll do it anyway

We're human

PROLOGUE

Silence exploded around them, echoing in their ears with physical intensity and vibrating as though they'd been in the center of the world's worst thunderstorm.

Which, of course, they had been. Metaphorically speaking.

"Are they gone, now?" the girl whispered timidly.

Her mother smiled warmly under weary eyes. "Yes, darlin'. That's the last of 'em". To no one but herself she added, "Poor bastards" under her breath.

She took her daughter's hand and they walked together away from the carnage and into the sunlight.

CHAPTER ONE

The leaves rustled imperceptibly. There was no wind to speak of, and the air was heavy with heat.

The reek of hogs blended with the aroma of overturned soil and muddied up creek bottom, broken pine branches and the ever-present scent of the sun baking and broiling everything above ground.

Where the hogs had been looked like a war zone.

Shayla mentally kicked herself for being so inattentive. What if they'd been on the inside of the enclosure instead of the outside when the hogs barreled into it and destroyed everything they didn't inhale and then back out again- bristly, odiferous tornadoes? She shuddered to think of the sharp hooves, the crusty tusks. She felt Athalie's tiny hand in hers and vowed to be more careful.

The hogs were a problem. They were not indigenous, they were feral. And very fertile. They had precious few natural enemies and the countryside was overrun with them. They laid waste everywhere they went and they went everywhere. They also carried disease and could be aggressive.

So there was no closed season on hogs- and no limit, and no restrictions on how they were hunted. In areas where they were particularly thick, large enclosures were built of extremely stout wire panels- big as a small barn yard. They'd be stocked with food and the hogs would run in, eat up, and run out- they were very smart and very wary but very greedy and very hungry.

Once they were accustomed to this routine, a trip would be set to close the gate and they'd be trapped and summarily executed. The smaller ones could be butchered, but the larger ones were too tough and rank.

Shayla felt only a little sorry for them. They were still fellow beings on the planet and they were being set up for a quick and inglorious ending. But there really was nothing else for it- they were destroying not only human habitation and agriculture, but all the native plants as well as fouling all the ground water they came in contact with.

She and Athalie had been hunting bramble berries on the 490 acres adjacent to theirs. They had permission to do so and were aware that the hogs were being hunted in there- there was no mistaking or misinterpreting the late-night baying of the hog dogs and the firing of high powered rifles. But she hadn't known about the enclosure hunting. Now she did, and she wouldn't forget it.

Bramble hunting in itself is a little treacherous- the brambles have thorns, of course. They also harbor snakes which have to be watched for- most of the time the snakes are gone before anyone knows they are there, but just in case, it paid to be mindful.

So they *had* been paying attention. Just not to large enclosures of hog wire, which to be fair, were hellaciously difficult to see what with all the other underbrush and thorny viney things. And that's why the hogs went in there at all. It didn't look too terribly threatening.

When the hogs came thundering through, Shayla had grabbed Athalie and sandwiched her small body between herself and the trunk of a huge sweet gum tree that was by luck alone on the outside side of the enclosure.

It never failed to amaze her that a huge herd of hundred-plus pound hogs and their many and various babies could be not there one minute, fill the entire universe the next, and be gone without a trace the third.

She and Athalie waited till their breathing returned to normal, gathered up their bramble berry baskets which had survived unbelievably upright and unscathed, and carefully made their way home to make a cobbler for dinner. It was supposed to be just for dessert, but considering their recent brush with calamity, it seemed fitting to eat only dessert for dinner, just this once.

CHAPTER TWO

The leaves rustled imperceptibly. There was no wind to speak of, and the air was heavy with heat.

Fireflies flickered on and off, on and off in a never-ending cacophony of complex communication that only looked like the worlds' tee-tiniest fireworks.

Suddenly, as if on cue, they stopped and the night was black velvet pierced by static stars, the back drop awaiting the actors' next scene.

For years people had said, half-jokingly, that Mother Earth would one day just shake us off like so many fleas; shake off the parasites that had pestered her and prodded her and drained her and sullied her.

For years there had been warnings- more storms, more droughts, more fires and more floods. More tornadoes in alleys that weren't tornado alley, more hurricanes that weren't following the usual hurricane routes. The weather was shifting and the planet couldn't adapt quickly enough.

Thunder rumbled in the distance in menace or warning. Or both.

Shayla sat on her porch, rocking and watching the fireflies. The house was quiet; Athalie had gone to bed and through the open window Shayla heard the air quietly entering and exiting her daughter's lungs. She saw in her mind's eye the rise and fall of the light summer quilt, golden brown hair streaming haphazardly across the pillow, one set of pink-painted toes peeking out from the bottom of the covers, the other foot firmly resting on Olive, who snored in rhythm with Athalie's breathing.

Olive had been dumped by the side of the road. Athalie had been playing outside and heard the car stop up on the bridge, heard the pitiful 'yipe' followed by the squeal of tires as they easily outpaced the puppy running after them; so sure there had been a mistake- any minute now they'd realize it and come back.

Running to the road, visions of what would happen if another car came along or if the pup lost its footing on the bridge blocked out any punishment she'd be given for venturing outside their gate. With a radar reserved for mothers and other youngsters, Athalie picked out the tiny ball of dirt-colored fur huddled miserably in the weeds, scooped her up against her chest and high-tailed it back to the house. Her hope was that there was some rule (like the rule about food dropped on the floor) that lightened the punishment if you were up on the road for less than five seconds. And she hoped for extra points for saving a life.

Shayla just sighed and shook her head. She didn't have to pretend to be angry about Athalie being on the road by herself; that made her very angry and anxious, and she told Athalie so. But she understood why she did it. She would've done it herself today at age 35, or thirty years ago at age 5.

Olive turned out to be a dog of many heritages-part spaniel, part terrier, part hound, part retriever, all heart; and 100% of that heart belonged to Athalie.

"Olive? Why would you name a dog 'Olive'? You don't even *like* ollves".

"Why not?"

There was no arguing with this reasoning because "why not?" was the primary driver of their lives.

When Shayla had announced that she was buying up a little piece of land with no more than a deer camp shack on it (calling it a 'cabin' would've been a huge compliment) her friends and family were appalled. She had a lovely apartment in town, close to work and all the comforts of a civilized life- movie theaters, grocery stores, restaurants, the mall. There was covered parking, they reminded her- *reserved* covered parking. "Why would you give all that up to go live in the woods like a hillbilly?"

"Why not?"

She had tried once to explain it in more than those two words to one of her co-workers; to explain how it made her head hurt to not ever be somewhere quiet, made her eyes hurt to not ever be somewhere dark, made her heart hurt to not ever be somewhere surrounded only by nature no matter which window she looked out of. He had looked at her like she was kidding him, the start of a smile on his face. When there was no punch line, he stammered something along the lines of, "Well, have fun with that" and beat a hasty retreat, making a mental note to check her name off the list of chicks he was planning on asking out.

The land was close enough to commute to work- only about 30 miles outside town and with the roads in between lacking both traffic lights and slow speed limit cities, it actually took 30 minutes. When she lived in town it would take her that long to get to work in the mornings past a dozen traffic lights, three school zones and a railroad crossing even though it was only 5 miles.

Even so, most of the people she knew were horrified that she'd even consider moving 'so far away'.

It was on a one lane country road, ten acres that had been carved out of 500 acres of deer lease that no one in the family wanted anymore. The idea, the family attorney had said, was that they could sell 10 acres and the 'house' for more per acre because of the 'improvements' and then try to find an investor and/or developer to buy up the rest.

With the current economy, no one had been interested in either one till she came along and made them an offer- since her credit was only passable thanks to her recent divorce (more accurately, her ex-husband's spending habits that had been one of the main causes *of* the divorce), it was agreed that she would pay the owners direct and the attorney had written it up all clear and fair. With a simple interest rate and no fees or the usual bank falderal, her place would be...her place in ten years and the payment was still modest enough for her to be able to do some improvements. If she was very frugal and learned to do most of it herself.

She was game. She wanted more than what she had for her daughter. An apartment with covered parking is no legacy either financially or emotionally. She wanted a Home.

So they'd moved into the ramshackle 12 X 24 ft. structure that had been the clubhouse for generations of deer hunters. It took her most of a cringe-filled week to shovel out the sand, grit, clay, beer cans, Coke bottles, tobacco cans and whatnot from the floor and peel the various posters of almost-nekkid women, guns, and trophy kills (in a few special cases *all three* in the same photo) off the walls.

She used five gallons of bleach scrubbing it out- one gallon per 57 square feet. The kitchen area was actually not that bad since the only thing they'd done there was cook giant manly breakfasts and toss pizzas in the oven. The oven consumed three containers of Easy-Off. The fridge was summarily hauled to the dump and replaced with a $50 one off of Craig's List that had had marginally better care.

Shayla and Athalie settled into their new house. It was clean. It was snug. It was cozy. It was still not Home.

Even with the little propane heater glowing on a chilly winter evening and the bed covered in old quilts there was just something 'off' about it.

The woods were thick on their little ten acres and it took a while to get to the back. Shayla had gotten a machete at the Army/Navy store and was literally blazing a trail through the forest. The previous owners had run a new fence around the acreage she had purchased when they decided to sell it, so there was no fear of getting lost but the foliage grows overnight in this part of the country and fences become invisible very quickly.

Shayla was hacking through the underbrush and Athalie was behind her- always looking at flowers and caterpillars down below and birds and squirrels up above.

"Home, Mama".

Shayla stopped in mid-swing. "What?"

"Home, Mama. Over there".

Athalie pointed off to the left and there it was. Only about a dozen feet away was the remnants of an old log structure.

Being careful and cautious and wary of snakes, and scorpions, and wasps- the other creatures that enjoy a good shelter, Shayla and Athalie crept up to the door and pushed it open.

The door creaked, but opened easily.

The cabin was roughly the size of the deer lease shack. One single room with one of the shorter walls almost overcome with a native rock fireplace and hearth. Two narrow windows bracketed the fireplace. There were two identical windows on either side of the front door, matching windows and doors along the back wall and a window on the side opposite the fireplace.

Shayla wondered momentarily why it was so dark in the cabin when there were ample windows and then she realized- shutters. There were working shutters closed tight against all the windows. This was the original deer hunting shack, meant to be used sparingly and then closed off the rest of the time.

Still looking for anything with fangs or a stinger, she told Athalie to wait on the little porch and she went around the cabin opening up the shutters one by one.

Coming back to the front of the place, she stepped inside again.

It was a mess.

The roof appeared to be tight yet, which was astounding, and there were only a few spots where the chinking needed replacing, and of course all the windows had survived the years. But there were years and years of dust and rodent and bird droppings carpeting the floors made of...rock?

The floor had been laid like a rock patio- flat stone laid into a base of sand and clay (the two main ingredients of the soil around there). It was far from even, but at least there was no way it was rotten.

The next day she called the previous owners to ask about the old cabin and was told that yes, they were aware of it, but no one had thought about it in years. Once electricity and sewer had been run down the little country road, the 'new' cabin had been set right there up on the road and hooked up- the cost of running electric and water back to the 'old' cabin was nothing any of the family had wanted to tackle. It had been way cheaper to slap up the new structure where it was.

It changed nothing. In fact, the people she was buying the place from apologized that they had neglected to tell her about it and wanted to know if she needed any help hauling it all out of there or burning it.

"No, no no! I, ummm...I think I'll take my time and use the logs for firewood, maybe the windows for a greenhouse project and the rocks for...something. It's OK- I'll take care of it. Although it *would* have been nice to have been warned about such an eyesore," she added quickly and as snarkily as she could.

She hung up the phone, looked at Athalie and said, "Well, whatta ya know? We *are* Home, after all".

While they still officially lived in the shack up near the road, the cabin at the back of the place was now getting all the attention. Rummage sales, Craig's List, word of mouth, Goodwill, Habitat for Humanity, all the remnant and scratch and dent warehouses knew Shayla by name. While everyone else was scrounging for good deals on the new stuff, Shayla went straight to the back of the warehouses looking at what had been pulled out of old homes before demolition.

The short wall of the cabin became a half-galley kitchen. Five 2-foot wide mismatched free-standing lower cabinets lined the wall, a tiled plywood counter tying them together. The center one, under the window, housed an old fashioned porcelain deep double sink with no faucets and a hose underneath exited to the outside where one of the floor rocks had been. On one end, a Craig's List find- an old icebox. Open wooden shelves lined the entire wall up above and stored dishes and glasses. The lower cabinets were reserved for food.

Because there was precious little cabinetry in the shack up on the road, Shayla started storing most of her food in the log cabin. Always a thrifty shopper, she would buy double when on sale of items that would last and be versatile- baking mix, bulk pastas and rice, sugar and flour, spices, oatmeal, beans, as well as paper products, cleaning supplies plus bathroom and first aid items. Paper products were plastic-toted and duct-taped against rodents and stacked in the low loft above one end of the cabin. Food was sealed in canisters and large Tupperware from Goodwill and all the bottom cabinets were full.

There was a double iron-steaded bed in the center of the room with a big old mahogany buffet tight up against it. The buffet's drawers held pots, pans and other utensils.

During the day, the bed pillows lined up against the back of the buffet to make the world's comfiest sofa. Suspended from the rafters along half of the front wall was a brilliantly woven hammock that Athalie adored. It took some doing to convince Olive to try it, but her love for her human had persevered and now she didn't even hesitate before launching herself into it and flattening down till the swaying stopped.

Six 'under the bed drawers' with snapping covers were tucked under the bed and held their clothing.

Out the back door was a tiny porch- about 6 feet square, unlike the side to side and 8 foot deep front porch. After careful consideration and planning, Shayla and Athalie closed the back porch in using scrap lumber and shingles and a 'sample' window that had been part of a new home building display. There was enough room for a sawdust toilet, a wash stand and pitcher, and a camping-style shower set up.

On the roof was a 20 gallon black plastic container that heated water when the sun shone and opened into the shower.

Shayla learned to cook over a fire in the fireplace or outside, and at night they read by oil lamp light.

Most folks didn't even know about the cabin at the back of their place. Their closest friends knew about it and assumed that it was a pastime, a hobby, a type of weekend getaway for them...like a tree house.

No one would've dreamed that they lived there full time.

But why not?

When they'd divorced, Shayla had given up the big screen TV without so much as a raised eyebrow- she never watched it anyway. She and Athalie made up stories and acted out plays and read books either out on the porch or sitting on the high pine needle-cushioned creek bank while dragonflies wove invisible webs in the air.

If company came out, which was a rare occurrence in the winter without the ready comfort of central heat and an absolute non-event in the summer since there wasn't air conditioning in either structure and most people thought they would die without it; they did whatever entertaining they did from the shack on the front of the property.

The one with the electricity and flush toilet.

And the refrigerator. Shayla stood up and considered whether or not she was thirsty enough for a cold drink to traipse the few hundred feet through the deep woods in the dark for the pitcher of sweet tea that she'd left in the shack.

The thunder rumbled again, closer and more threatening.

No, she decided; perhaps a drink from the pitcher of water on the kitchen counter would be just fine.

She went into the house and the rocking chair eerily kept rocking for a few minutes, first from the momentum of her getting up, and then from the breeze catching it just right. Finally it slowed and then stopped.

Looked like a storm brewing.

Shayla latched the door even though she knew no one was out there.

CHAPTER THREE

The leaves rustled imperceptibly. There was no wind to speak of, and the air was heavy with heat.

Shayla tossed and turned in her bed while Olive paddled in her sleep, chasing squirrels in her dreams and causing the hammock to sway as though the wind in Shayla's dream had found a way outside her head.

It was a recurring dream. In it Athalie was a tiny baby, always a tiny baby. Shayla would dream she'd woken up and Athalie was missing. Frantic, she'd search the house and then run out the front door to see a woman walking down the road carrying her child. Just the back of the woman. Something seemed familiar about her hair, her shape, the way she walked, and even her clothing reminded her of someone she couldn't quite remember.

She wasn't afraid- she just wanted her baby back.

So she ran after the woman, calling for her to stop but as in many dreams, she tried to yell but nothing came out but a raspy whisper. Frustrated but still not frightened, she ran faster and finally caught up to the woman who started turning around and...

23

...Shayla never did see who the woman was but the baby wasn't Athalie. The baby was herself as she'd seen in a hundred photos of herself as a baby.

And that's when she'd wake up. Every time.

She startled awake to her cell phone's incessant humming; she set it to vibrate after Athalie was asleep- living in one room required some extra thought at times. As she answered it she noted the time- 11:30pm. Who ever?

It was her closest neighbor Tammy, who lived up the road about a half mile. Tammy lived with her husband Ray and their two kids Amber and Little Ray. Ray worked the oil field and was gone for three weeks and home for one, so three quarters of the time Tammy was a single mom just like Shayla. When Ray was gone Shayla and Tammy got together regularly to cook meals and let the kids play. Tammy babysat Athalie while Shayla worked and Shayla was a grownup Tammy could talk to after an entire day of being surrounded by little people.

They planted, tended, harvested and preserved a big vegetable garden together and together raised chickens for eggs and meat and goats for milk. Tammy and Ray had 20 acres that was only half wooded and had a big old barn so their place was perfect for all that. They were living in a double-wide for now, but they'd been saving up since they got married and within the next few years would be building their own house and paying cash.

When Ray was home, they'd invite Shayla and Athalie over for cookouts but Shayla only accepted about half the time. It was easy to feel like a fifth wheel even though they never did or said anything that would foster that notion. Shayla was ever so grateful that her neighbors were few but true.

Right at the moment, Tammy was a single mom- Ray had just left out the week before.

"Shayla? I'm so sorry to call this late! Are ya'll ok? The kids and I were all sound asleep when the storm hit- wind and rain and hail and then the sound of a freight train! I grabbed the kids and ran into bathroom- the whole house shook for what seemed like an hour! When it passed we opened the door and the house is OK but our barn is flat gone! All our big trees are down and by the trail of the wreckage it headed ya'lls way! I was so afraid you wouldn't answer!" Tammy stopped, breathless because she hadn't paused once during the entire outburst.

Shayla was still clearing sleepy cobwebs and the remnants of her dream from her head as she looked around and out the windows- nothing. Nothing was out of place on the porches or in the yard. Not a leaf out of place and it hadn't even rained at her house.

"We're OK, Tammy. We're OK. What about the goats? Were they in the barn?"

"No, thank heavens- I'd had the kids in town shopping and got home later than expected. They were crabby and hungry so I made dinner and put them straight to bed- I forgot all about locking the goats in the barn- they were still out in the pasture and they're OK- all accounted for but looking positively vexed that their supper dishes have disappeared." Tammy started laughing in spite of the circumstances.

"Tammy, you sure you're OK?"

"Yes, darlin', we're fine. I was just worried about ya'll. This weather keeps getting stranger and stranger all the time. Never know what it's going to do next. The kids are already back sound asleep, I'm pouring myself a thimbleful of Jack Daniels and I'm right behind 'em. I'll see you girls in the morning."

The cell phone went quiet. Athalie's hammock was still; Olive must've caught all the squirrels

in doggie dreamland because she'd stopped
paddling and her tail was quivering
rhythmically, wagging in her sleep.

Their cabin was safe and so were they...this
time.

Why would a tornado materialize out of thin air,
lay waste to a perfectly good barn and then
disappear like a herd of wild hogs?

Why not?

Shayla lay awake for a long time before nodding
off again.

CHAPTER FOUR

The leaves rustled imperceptibly. There was no wind to speak of, and the air was heavy with heat.

The weird and slightly dysfunctional spring weather morphed into an absolutely psychotic summer.

Like molecules heating over a Bunsen burner the weather map of the US flashed and sparked fast and erratic: tornadoes here, hurricanes there, flash floods followed by wildfires and vice versa, and none where they were expected.

The Southeast's marshes and swamplands dried up, leaving gators grounded and cranky, and snakes of all stripes slithered into anyplace with water and shade- human habitation was their obvious choice.

The Pacific Northwest was hazy with the smoke and ashes from not one but two volcanic eruptions, turning the lush rainforests gray with suffocation.

Down in the desert, the usually dry riverbeds were roiling and flooding; washing away century-old cacti and mesquite and leaving behind red mud and drowned rattlers.

The snow had never left the northlands at all. Folks from St. Louis north and from sea to sea waited first with the patience of Yankees accustomed to wildly variable planting dates, then with annoyance, then alarm as March turned into April...May...June...July and the snow kept falling.

The entire Breadbasket went to Hell in a hand basket. One tornado spawned another in a never-ending dervish and the storms that accompanied them were rainless but filled with savage lightening that ignited tinder dry fields and forests of standing firewood.

Farmers and firefighters, homeowners and first responders watched helplessly as huge balls of flame were carried aloft by the funnel clouds and dropped miles away; Mother Nature was at war with her parasites, and no matter how clever, the parasites would not win.

Shayla read by lamplight and listened with one ear, always now listened with one ear straining to hear the faintest shift in the atmosphere. Their woods were as dry as the rest; the normally emerald green forest was sickly yellow with dust and drought fatigue. Every day was hotter than the one before it, the sun rising angry and sullen, and as it arced across the sky it was more and more common to hear the sharp yet muffled "pop" of a pine bursting out of its bark- the sap brought to boiling.

The fireflies were frantic; blinking in response to the heat lightning that flashed silently, turning the cabin's interior into the world's un-trendiest disco.

Athalie murmured in her sleep, turned ever so slightly to plant her tiny foot even more firmly against Olive, who softly grunted, sighed and resumed snoring.

Shayla's book dropped into her lap, the pages fluttering in the breeze her breath made. In her dream, the pages of her book became butterflies gently flitting, then clouds scudding across the sky quickly, and then they were a river, whitecaps churning and bubbling, higher and wilder as the train bore down on them.

The train.

Before her eyes were fully open, Shayla had grabbed up Athalie with one hand and Olive with the other and dove under the heavy iron bedstead in the center of the room, clutching them both for dear life.

The night was suddenly darker than black, which made the flashes of lightning even brighter and more terrifying, striking so close

unimpressive   Sheri Dixon

the ozone burned their nostrils and their hair
stood on end.

The anguished tearing of trees being yanked
like weeds and cast aside by Thor's temper was
too much for her and she closed her eyes tight
against the fear.

Closer it came, and closer still, till the windows
in the cabin imploded and the logs groaned
with grief for their fallen comrades in the forest.

Shingles took flight in terror and disappeared
into the funnel, and the logs were strained to
their limits, twisting till the chinking crumbled
and evaporated in the wind that sucked all the
air out of their lungs

...and then it was over.

CHAPTER FIVE

The leaves rustled imperceptibly. There was no wind to speak of, and the air was heavy with heat.

The big heavy bedstead had stood firm in the center of the house; all the other furniture was twisted and clustered up against it, tilted and mangled on top of it, jammed and folded underneath it as though it had all crowded there for protection.

From the edge of one corner of the Salvador Dali-esque tableau came a quiet little scraping- hesitant at first and then more insistent until three bedraggled forms emerged- squeezing through the tiny space and unfolding once clear of their lumber and metal cocoon.

What none of them knew is that they had dived under the bed in one world and just a few brief moments later were coming out the other side of the looking glass...and none of their caterpillar ways would serve them now.

Now was the time to fly.

Shayla checked her pocket and found to her relief that her cell phone was still there. The time was 11:30 pm. Crossing her fingers that Tammy was still awake, she called her neighbor.

"Hello?"

"Tammy- this is Shayla. We've been hit by a tornado. Are ya'll ok?"

"Wait. What? I thought for a minute you said you were hit by a tornado, darlin'."

"Tammy- yes! That's exactly what I said! We're OK but the cabin is a mess- all the windows are out and the furniture may be a total loss except for the bed. The ones who count are ok, though- Athalie and Olive are fine, and I'm fine."

"Sweet Baby Jesus, darlin'- the wind ain't even strong enough to blow over a feather here! I'm headed pick you up. You have to come here to the house for the night at least- we'll worry about your clean up in the morning". And the phone went silent.

Shayla and Athalie moved slowly, unsure of their new wings and as if their feet wouldn't hold them up anymore. Mechanically they searched for and gathered the remnants of civility- extra clothes, a bit of food, their toothbrushes that were unaccountably still in the upright glass on the bathroom sink.

Neither of them had shed a tear...yet. Neither of them had spoken to each other...yet.

They clutched their things and walked out the front door and down the path to the little house on the road. They didn't have flashlights but didn't need them. The moon was full and brilliant.

Turning around, they gazed back at the cabin.

"We're still invisible", Athalie said quietly.

And so they were. The trees in front of the cabin were all still standing and barely a needle ruffled, while everything behind it was...gone. Not knocked over. Not piled like toothpicks.

Gone.

From here Shayla could see that although it was a mess, the cabin was still habitable and still home. The roof was mostly intact- In the moonlight she could see just missing shingles but the decking appeared to be there. The windows and doors were, of course, history, but those could be replaced little by little as she could...just like she'd been doing all along. The chinking could be replaced and the entire interior cleaned up and out.

Nothing had been new and perfect to begin with, so that was a plus.

Shayla hugged Athalie to her tightly- as tightly as she'd held her during the tornado. "I think being invisible is a very good thing", she whispered to her daughter, and Olive bumped them with her nose and smiled a dog smile in agreement.

The three of them sat on the porch of the deer lease shack and waited for Tammy, unwilling to go inside. Even though it had been untouched by the tornado, the shack still felt less welcoming than the cabin.

CHAPTER SIX

The leaves rustled imperceptibly. There was no wind to speak of, and the air was heavy with heat.

Sitting in Tammy's living room, freshly showered and in clean clothes, bowls of consoling ice cream in front of the kids and glasses of consoling wine in front of Tammy and Shayla, they all watched the TV together. When your cabin is rearranged by a tornado during the night, breakfast is allowed to be somewhat unconventional.

They were watching the news...or maybe the weather. Turned out they were watching the weather because it *was* the news.

Nothing about the tornado that changed the shape of Shayla and Athalie's life- that was small potatoes and not worth mentioning to most folks. The talk was of the storm. The Storm.

The Solar Storm that had silently rolled across North America, Central America, South America just after sunrise.

The Solar Storm that changed the face of a large part of the earth on the heels of the actually pretty tiny-in-retrospect tornado that rearranged Shayla's cabin came as a surprise to everyone.

Everyone except the scientists who had been warning of exactly that for years; had even pinpointed when it was most likely to occur, and who were now unaccountably in deep shit because it had happened just as they had warned...but no one had taken them seriously and this was now somehow their fault.

And now they got their 15 minutes of fame. Now they got to go on all the TV shows, all the radio shows, all the webcasts that they had tried to get access to before. Well, not the webcasts- those were already gone.

The TV and radio shows were rife with charts and diagrams all showing what a solar storm is, what a solar storm does, and the relative chain of events that no one could do a single thing to change.

There was no weapon big enough, no chemical strong enough, no Hollywood star or Special Ops team that could valiantly sacrifice themselves within it in a glorious explosion of patriotism and save the Americas now.

It was too late.

It was too late before it even happened because there was nothing they could've done to prevent it.

But they surely could've prepared for it.

And yet, they didn't.

Oh, for sure the nearly guaranteed coming of a solar storm was big enough, flashy enough, and most importantly marketably glamorous enough for the big corporations to fool with. But it also got all balled up with other weather-related things...things that screamed of climate change, the bugaboo Global Warming stuff of tree huggers and alarmists. So it got no air time and no affirmation.

So here they were and the scientists had the unenviable task of laying out the probable and unchangeable timeline.

Vincent McLean now sat in front of the cameras; shoved ingloriously there by circumstance and looking like he hadn't slept in weeks. Disheveled and exhausted, his appearance was not a dramatic ploy and not an act- he'd been literally plucked from his office at the university in between classes to be the Local Expert on solar storms.

He blinked back at the blinking light on the front of the TV camera, tapped his notes on the desk in front of them in a moment of organization both physical and mental, and then proceeded to give the most important lecture of his career.

"At the time of the event most home and simple business computers (anything that depends on the internet) will become inoperable, as most of you have already found out.

Within the first 8 hours, there will be some disruption of cell and landline services as the towers and satellites became erratic- call who you need to now because you may not have another chance for a very long time.

After 24 hours there will be pretty much no electrical service to ... anything depending on the main power grids. The teeny computer chips in cars will still work, but not the pumps to the gas stations. The cell phones will (maybe) still work, but not the chargers.

Without access to gasoline and diesel, all the stores depending on daily deliveries will start seeing empty shelves, but in the case of meat, dairy, produce and frozen items it won't matter- none of that will be cooled anyway. Of

course there will be no lights on in the store and
the cash registers won't ring anything up.

After three days, the satellites broadcasting for
TV and radio will be mostly crippled, but no one
will notice because the TV's and radios will have
already been silenced before that. The
emergency broadcast networks will start going
fidgety.

A week into the event, back-up power supplies
like generators that are the safety net for
businesses and hospitals will be straining to
maintain and running out of their own power."

"And by day 30", Vincent said quietly while
staring directly into the camera, "Everything will
be dark and enveloped in silence."

There was a sudden uncomfortable silence in
the TV studio.

Pert and perky anchorwoman Misty Barton
cleared her throat and looked optimistic. She
distractedly patted her blond locks, licked her
'Naked Ambition' lipstick and straightened her
teal silk blouse just a bit- tugging it down taut
over her made-for-TV bosoms. "Well, now isn't
that exciting! Sounds like a big ol' campout is in
order! So we have about a week to stock up and
get ready for this total shutdown- we have less

warning for a hurricane or ice storm! So when will everything be fixed?"

Professor McLean looked at her with a mixture of sadness and exasperation. "Fixed? You want to know when the entire electrical grid for an entire continent will be fixed after a major solar event?" and he started laughing in a completely non-humorous way.

Looking confused, Misty dropped just a bit of her on-camera persona and a hint of testiness broke through the velvet veneer of her carefully modulated speaking voice. "Well, yes darlin'-fixed. See, I'm a judge at the Missy Bible Belt Competition next month down here on the Gulf...anyone who's anyone will be there- event of the year, you know! It'll be all up and back to normal by then, right?"

The laughing stopped abruptly. Vincent looked at her like she was speaking a foreign language. Thus far, he had been conveying information in a professional manner like the professional "that he was. For years and years, study after study regarding the history of coronal mass ejections had been published and promptly mocked by just about everyone.

People who had seen Y2K come and go without their computers crashing. People who thought every single winter storm disproved 'Global Warming'. People who seriously and smugly denied evolution by sneering, "If we came from monkeys, how come there are still monkeys???" and high-fived each other in a very "Take THAT, Mr. Science!" way.

People who did believe them tended to use the knowledge to further cement themselves into corners of paranoia and regularly confused coronal mass ejections (CME) with electro-magnetic pulses (EMP), refusing to acknowledge the difference even when it was pointed out to them over and over again: that the only things they had in common were they came from the sky and 'would mess a bunch of shit up'.

Now it had happened. Now it was real. There had been precious little preparation because they hadn't been taken seriously and now it was suddenly the scientists' fault that everyone had been too busy watching Survivor Madagascar and Tots in Tiaras and even people in the government had been too busy being distracted by things that compared to *this*, mattered very little.

He tried.

He took a deep breath and really, truly tried.

He tried to calmly tell her when it would be fixed.

But he just couldn't do it. Something inside him snapped.

"Missy Bible Belt pageant???! What are you, a complete imbecile? Do you actually comprehend the news you chirp at us every day or just recite it and smile? No, my dear- there will be no Missy Bible Belt pageant down on the Gulf this year. Or next year. Or the year after. Because you see, my blond blow-dried fluff ball, what happened last night IS the event of the year- actually the event of the century, and it's a pretty young century but I'm reasonably sure this, this right here, is gonna win Event of the Century."

"You want to know when it'll be 'back to normal'. How about Decades. Is that good enough for you? Decades. It will take a minimum of two years to even get where we can *start* replacing electrical transformers and then another decade or so to even make a dent in replacing them all. The economic impact of this will be enormous. The human impact will be profound. For the foreseeable future, society will have to learn damn quickly how to function without the niceties we've grown accustomed to having at the flip of a switch or the turn of a key or the press of a button. There. Is that concise enough for you to understand?"

"IF, and it's a big IF, people can stop their lives in mid-stream and focus on helping each other in their time of need instead of being complete selfish bastards, we just might get through this and out the other side a better species."

"I'm an astrophysicist. I've dedicated my entire life to studying the sun and its patterns of behavior through historical records and all the delicate and intricate instrumentation and measurements mankind has invented over the last hundred years. I've recorded all of it along with the other astrophysicists and we've relayed the information on to you- our fellow travelers on this beautiful green and blue dot in the Universe. And for the most part, no one has cared. Do you care now?"

"So here's what I recommend, Buttercup. I recommend you call your loved ones before the phones stop working. You stock up on supplies before the stores run out and/or close. You gather people together - friends and neighbors and family members and you share. You share food and you share knowledge and you re-align your values and let go of the *things* you think you need to grab tight to the *people* you truly need. You stay calm and collected and if we can all do that we'll come out the other side of this relatively unscathed and undoubtedly better for it.

"Or, we can all run around panicking and shooting each other for 'valuables' that are now totally worthless. We can 'every man for themselves' Cowboy and Rambo ourselves right out of existence. Our choice, I guess".

He sighed, mumbled "Ah...fuck it", shook his head wearily and walked out of the studio.

CHAPTER SEVEN

The leaves rustled imperceptibly. There was no wind to speak of, and the air was heavy with heat.

The ice cream puddled in the bowls and the wine had cooled to room temperature. All were untouched.

The TV station had quickly switched back to the regularly-scheduled laugh-tracked sit-com re-run and it was as if the broadcast they had just watched had never happened.

"Soooo...we don't have school today?" Little Ray was always that one in the crowd who could lighten the mood.

Tammy and Shayla looked at each other for a long moment.

"No, Ray- no school today. I want you and the girls to go feed and water the goats; I'm gonna call your daddy and see when he'll be home. Then we're going to the store."

When the children were out of earshot, Shayla shook her head, "Holy shit. We need a plan. You call Ray and I'll take inventory here. I've got a pretty good idea of what we've got at our place and I'll add that to the list. Be ready to go in 30 minutes."

Like all plans, this one turned out nothing like originally intended.

Ray was working in North Dakota and knew nothing about what had happened other than the 'goddamn computers weren't working' at the worksite. Within five minutes, his truck was fueled up and he was on the road...but it was a very long way home. He promised to be home as soon as he could make it, and he promised that he would make it if he had to walk.

Tammy hung up the phone and stared into Shayla's eyes. "A voice. He's just a tiny little voice in a box that won't work after a few days' time. Then what?" she implored. "Then what?" she repeated in a whisper. Shayla smiled at her friend. "Then he'll be a big ol' bear hug when he gets home. He's going to get home, darlin'. I know it. All we have to do is keep 'home' here till then".

After looking over their inventory list, the women were encouraged and decided they didn't need to go to the store after all. Between them they had a fair supply of paper and cleaning products, basic first aid items, and dry, canned and bulk food. All they'd gain by fighting their way through the mess that was sure to be the grocery store would be perishables that wouldn't matter in a few days anyhow.

They each had a vehicle, and living in hurricane territory they both had full tanks- you just never let your tank get below half around here so you could get a few hundred miles between you and a nasty storm at a moment's notice. They'd save their gas for emergencies.

Where else did they need to go? They thought about going to the bank, but considering what they both had in their checking accounts combined was under $1,000 it really wasn't worth the hassle. If and when the grid went back up again, their money would either be there...or not. Shayla had no savings, and Tammy and Ray had a 401k with his company- that was out of reach now anyway.

"Wait. No. No, no no no." Tammy exhaled in protest.

"Our house money. All of our house money- we HAVE to get that out of the bank and spend it...today".

The road into town was strangely quiet.

Once in town, it got a little crazy, but still not bad. The grocery store was over-run. The gas station lines were around the block and growing. The drive- through at the small local bank was closed and the parking lot was full. It was just after 9am.

Inside the bank, people were waiting with a bizarre combination of patience and intensity. The tellers manned their stations stoically and the bank manager came out of her office and faced the customers. "Look- we're a very small branch and our main location has told us that there would be no more armored trucks running. What we have in the vault is what we have. We've run the numbers and we have enough money to close everyone's accounts...up to $10,000."

Most of the townspeople didn't have that much in the bank, but a few were horrified and angry- all their life savings were there and it damn sure was more than $10,000. Ray and Tammy's house fund had over $50,000 in it.

Before the mood got out of hand, Shayla spoke up. "This is a strange day for all of us, and we need to re-think everything- how we live and how we do business, how we act towards each other and what is valuable. Do any of us really want more than $10,000 cash in or around our homes during uncertain times? Really? I believe just making public that that's the limit will actually make our community safer in the next few months".

Grudgingly, everyone agreed. The bank manager took care of each customer herself in her office for privacy. Finally, Shayla and Tammy left the bank. In the truck, Shayla said, "OK, Thelma- where to?" Tammy laughed and said, "Well, Louise...I reckon all the big name brand chain stores will be insane. How about the Habitat for Humanity ReStore?"

Just as suspected, every grocery store, Wal-Mart, gas station, liquor store and pharmacy was absolutely teeming with people trying to buy enough of everything to last for as long as possible. The crowds were mostly civil, if anxious; compounding the issue was that at least 90% of all employees were not at work- they were all doing the same thing with and for their own families.

The children were wide-eyed in the back seat- life had certainly taken a strange turn literally overnight. This was something they would remember for a long time- the Day Everyone In the World Went Shopping at the Same Time.

The parking lot of the Restore was just about empty. There was one car in the lot and it belonged to the lone employee at the register. He looked up in mild surprise and asked if he could help them find anything; forced normalcy. Tammy laughed and said, "Yes- we need everything!"

And they worked their way through the store
and warehouse, neatly and tightly piling as
much as they could think of into the back of the
truck and the old stock trailer they normally
used to transport hay and goats- new windows
for Shayla's house and replacement shingles,
and as Tammy said everything for the house she
and Ray would be building- windows, doors,
shingles, plumbing and electrical supplies,
faucets and light switches, light fixtures and
cabinets, paint, trim lumber, toilets, a shower
enclosure and from the very back of the
warehouse an old claw foot tub. That went into
the trailer last because it took all of them
heaving and hauling to wrangle it into place.

The total came to $8,700. Tammy gave him
$9,000 and told him to keep the change.

By the time they were headed home, the
parking lots that had been so full just a few
hours before were almost deserted, evidence of
the stores' now barren shelves straggled out
the doors and faded into the deserted parking
spaces- broken packaging, cartons and boxes,
even some of the shelving from the aisles
leaked out of the open doorways dejectedly
and flowed half-heartedly into the street.

"Wow", whispered Amber to no one in particular. "Are you sure we have enough food, Mama?"

Tammy looked pointedly at Shayla for a split second, and then smiled into the rear view mirror at the row of worried little faces in the back seat. "Yes, darlin's- we have plenty of food and everything else we need. We may run short of a few things we *want*, but we'll always have all that we *need*. I promise you that."

"But Mama? How will we be sure that no one comes and takes *our* stuff? We don't have lots of guns like the people on all the survival TV shows have", Little Ray asked, serious demeanor masking his fear.

"I know how", whispered Athalie.

"We all need to be invisible".

CHAPTER EIGHT

The leaves rustled imperceptibly. There was no wind to speak of, and the air was heavy with heat.

The neighbors who had been friends before had become Family and they were holding their first family meeting. Two young women and three young children faced each other solemnly and thoughtfully, assessing their situation.

The house was quiet; quieter than what most people used to think of as quiet.

Quiet yesterday meant that the TV was off, and maybe the lights. But in the background always hummed things never thought about- refrigerators and computers and heating/cooling systems.

Quiet today meant...quiet.

They could only guess whether or not the TV stations were still broadcasting, because the TV itself wasn't working anymore. Tammy called Ray again for a few minutes- as long as she could plug the phone into the car's lighter to charge it and as long as the cell towers were transmitting they promised to call each other for five minutes a day...just to touch base. Just to touch.

Ray had made it to Kansas before needing more fuel, and had been fortunate enough to find a farmer with a diesel tank on his ranch who had sold him enough to fill the tank...for $50 a gallon. He was sticking to smaller two-lane roads and skirting wide around any big cities and had had no problems so far. His work truck was an older model that sported more than a few dents and scrapes and it seemed held together with the black dirt of North Dakota over the red clay of Texas. Ray himself was unshaven and rumpled in his old jeans and work shirt; oil-stained work cap on his head.

He wasn't hauling anything of monetary worth and wasn't driving anything flashy. He looked as harried and hurried as 90% of everyone on the road- people who were traveling as quickly as they could, not with their valuables in their pockets but headed come hell or high water home to the valuables in their hearts.

Tammy reconfigured her home to match Shayla's cabin- something she had been prepared to do, but never had to do until now- run the household without electricity for more than a few hours. Both the antique lanterns that had been scattered around the house 'decoratively' and camping lanterns they'd stocked up on were called into service to provide light once the sun went down, but even though they had gallons of oil and yards of wicking and thousands of matches, they used only what they needed- not a drop more.

When they went to bed that first night after pulling the truck and trailer into the rudimentary barn Ray had hastily built after the big barn had blown away, they were acutely aware of how much today had been different from yesterday...and it was a strange and unsettling thought that for the next months, every single day would be different from the one before.

Every day they'd plan to not use any outside energy or depend on any outside forces; they'd use what they still had sparingly and carefully, and be thankful for what they had while it still worked and right up until it didn't anymore.

 And then they'd go on without it.

No looking back.

They knew many people were on the move- trying to get to family or trying to get out of the big cities that were heavy on people and light on resources.

They knew that they were vulnerable- not because they didn't have a Man on site or a shed full of guns to use against others, but because they had stuff. Food and medical supplies and a well with a hand pump and potable water...the stuff of life.

The history books and Hollywood glorify armed confrontation, pre-emptive aggression, the Art of War, when the actual Art of War is to not even show up on the radar; the actual Art of War is avoidance and lying low until the threat is over.

So their assignment as of now was to become invisible.

Tammy and Ray didn't have much extended family, and those they did have were scattered over the South- some in Louisiana, some in Alabama, and a rogue nephew over in Austin. All were folks with the same mindset and temperament as themselves- after an initial quick phone call to be sure everyone was alright, they just dug in for the long haul. The nephew had his own network of friends in the city, and if you had to be stranded inside a big city during a disaster Austin was about as good as you could get.

Very progressive and environmentally sensitive, for several decades the Austonians had been encouraged to grow gardens, have backyard poultry, and invest in alternative energy with tax breaks for those who participated. Since there is very little 'wire distance' between the energy source and the battery bank and/or inverters of a home solar or wind set-up, and the main grid vulnerability in a solar storm is miles and miles of long distance wires 'frying', all of those small independent energy banks would continue to work.

People who had been teased about not being able to power up huge houses filled with electricity-guzzling toys were now the only ones with working toys at all.

But they didn't gloat, for the most part.

With Ray working the oil field, and Tammy being a stay at home mom, they really didn't socialize much or often and except for the lady who made the mail run every day, no one really knew where the gate to their place was. The gate itself was not fancy- just an old iron gate bracketed by cheap cattle panels. There was an ancient combination lock and chain that they'd only ever used when they were gone overnight. They yanked out the mailbox, locked the gate and swept over the truck tracks and their footprints with branches.

The house was invisible from the road, and if all they used were a few oil lamps and small fires for heating and cooking, their goal of invisibility was assured.

Shayla's place was more complex.

The shack sat right up on the road. It didn't contain anything of value, but it would attract attention.

Their choices seemed to be 'burn it down' or 'use it as a wayside stop for weary travelers'.

They took it to a vote.

Tammy and Amber voted to burn it down.

Shayla and Little Ray voted to use it as a wayside stop.

Athalie thought about it very seriously for a few moments, then said, "Wayside stop as long as people are nice. If they start wrecking stuff, we'll burn it down."

So they put some food and some water and some basic first aid supplies- a tube of antibiotic cream, a few Tylenol, some band aids- on the table in the unlocked shack.

They posted a sign on the inside wall that read-

Here is safety

Just for tonight

Take what we offer

Leave what you can

Trust the shadows

CHAPTER NINE

The leaves rustled imperceptibly. There was no wind to speak of, and the air was heavy with heat.

Tammy stirred fitfully in the tree stand just within sight of the shack.

Back in the day, the previous owners had had a deer feeder just below this stand and had fed the deer all year long. Just before dawn on opening day of hunting season, they'd stagger out of the lease shack after a night of playing cards and drinking beer, loudly shushing each other, pee off the porch and into the weeds, then precariously climb into the tree stand and valiantly 'hunt' the deer that had been basically trained to come for breakfast.

The tree stand hadn't been used for many years, and multiple vines (poison ivy, Virginia Creeper, kudzu and green briar) had woven up and around it till it was completely invisible unless you knew it was there.

The only reason Shayla had discovered it involved Olive and a stray cat who scrambled up the tree and then tiptoed along the outer edge of the stand, outlining it with every paw-step. One second it wasn't there, and the next it was in clear view…it was all a matter of perspective and association.

They all took turns off and on during the daylight hours keeping a watch over the shack and those who used it.

The first nine days there was a steady stream of visitors even though their road was not a main thoroughfare; people were taking the back ways out of the area. All were respectful, if stressed. They were those who had somewhere to go…if they could get there. They used the shack as somewhere to rest that wasn't the back seat of their car; somewhere the kids could have a semi-normal night's sleep. Mostly families, some couples, a few single people…all ate the food and drank the water, appreciated the washing basin and soap, spent the night and moved on after tidying up after themselves.

Those who could replaced the food, and a few left a few dollars and a thank you note.

On the tenth day, Tammy tried calling Ray three times before setting the phone in a drawer and closing it with finality. "Well, no more of that", she said matter-of-factly and with a false cheerfulness. She stared at the closed drawer as though she'd folded Ray himself up and closed him in there and for a minute she wished she had- at least she'd know that he was safe. She'd know where he was.

Ray had made it halfway through Oklahoma before running out of fuel and running out of luck in finding any. He'd traded the truck for a bicycle and a backpack.

After that there were more people on foot than not down their little road, and more people who looked like they didn't have anywhere to go, but nowhere to stay, either.

More and more of them were women with children, alone.

These they watched with interest and intent. Once darkness settled over the woods, Shayla and Tammy would call softly from outside-announcing themselves so as not to frighten the visitors...especially if they had weapons tucked in their packs yet within reach overnight.

Visitors who traveled with firearms strapped defiantly on the outside of their clothing were left to themselves to spend the night and then move on undisturbed- not out of fear, but because Tammy and Shayla wanted nothing to do with anyone who was overtly aggressive or outwardly confident.

The actual Art of War is avoiding it in the first place.

Once announced and invited in, the women would talk to the travelers- find out where they were from and where they were going. About half had a destination in mind and were happy for the place to stay but eager to be off in the morning. About half had no idea where they were headed but they had nothing to go back to.

Half of those with nowhere to go were running scared and stubborn. They were pissed at no one and everyone and resentful that their 'life was over'. Their kids mirrored their fear and bleak attitudes. These women never left anything to replace what they used and never said 'thank you'. Shayla and Tammy wished them well and off they went the next morning; running away and looking like the victims they would most likely become. Shayla and Tammy always tried to soothe them and try to get them to center themselves and make a calm and definitive plan for themselves, but it never worked.

Once they had crossed over into 'flight and flee-everything is bad' mode, there was no going back for them. Some just didn't know better; they'd never encountered anything in their lives that would have forced them to even have to think up a Plan B. Some had been too trusting in outside forces to take care of them no matter what- a rich husband, a loving god, a compassionate government.

Strength and happiness come from within- they can't be purchased and painted on or prayed into being.

The other half were calm and sensible and aware that life as they knew it was over for the foreseeable future and pragmatic about making do as best they could.

Because really? There was no other alternative that would keep their families safe.

These were the women they invited to stay. To become Shadows like themselves.

The theory was that the best way to wait out the initial turmoil after 'the end of the world' would be to be invisible and let the rest of the world work out the messy details.

That didn't mean turning their backs on others, and that's what they were doing- forming a community of people who understood that the future did not lie in the past and who believed the future could never be safe if it was born of violence.

The women who chose to stay were generally pretty well organized to begin with- some had a shelter of sorts with them, tents or large tarps, sleeping bags and rudimentary camping gear.

They used their own shelters to begin with, and used Shayla and Athalie's house as a template for their own cabins- rock floors, log walls, mud and clay chinking.

The new cabins were tucked here and there in the shallow hollows between the rolling hills of the forest so from almost every single angle even the roofs were hidden from view.

The roofs themselves were problematic until one of the women recalled watching thatchers at work in Europe and they experimented with different materials and patterns until they got it right.

The entire cabin building process was slow going with only hand tools and elbow grease, but they just worked at it every day as best they could.

They got up when it was light and went to bed when it was dark, ate when they were hungry and rested when they were tired.

It wasn't as if any of them were on a time clock anymore.

Tammy startled awake as the door to the shack closed with a muffled 'thud'. Through the window she could see the current visitor wasn't a woman alone or with children. Something about his silhouette was familiar though, and when she saw the bike parked outside the door she knew.

She was out of the tree and inside the shack with no cognizance of the space in between, through the door and into Ray's arms before he was aware she was there.

"Oh lordy, Tammy- I got to the gate and it was locked and the place looked abandoned! I came up here to see if Shayla knew where you and the kids had gone but she's not here, either. I've never felt so alone in all my life".

"For what? Thirty seconds?" Tammy laughed. But she hadn't turned loose of him, either.

"I told you I'd be home. Bet you don't even have dinner cooked for me", Ray frowned in mock anger at her while stoking her cheek tenderly.

And they walked home hand in hand and were greeted by two very happy children, and all in time for dinner.

The bike was left leaning dejectedly against the shack.

CHAPTER TEN

The leaves rustled imperceptibly. There was no wind to speak of, and the air was heavy with heat.

Days ran into weeks ran into months. The Shadows had been busy building their community and didn't much worry about what was going on 'outside'.

The garden and livestock at Tammy and Ray's place fed the small extended family- other than Tammy and Shayla there were six women and their children for a total of nine adults and fifteen children ranging in age from less than a year old to fourteen.

Two dozen people living silently in the woods supplementing their 'tame' foods with game and wild plants and they were fine.

Although they had Ray's old .22 and plenty of ammunition, they preferred silent harvest of meat using snares and by fishing.

One of the women was a nurse, and one was a teacher. One was an ol' hippie and one a master gardener. Everyone learned from everyone else- even the adults from the children.

Every so often Ray would go into town for a few supplies as well as any news. He always made sure to look on the verge of desperation and paid in crumpled single dollar bills or pocket change. He told the locals that Shayla and Athalie had left right after everything fell apart and it was just his family and him- and they were out of food and money and hard-scrabble scavenged for everything they had.

The initial months there was precious little to be had in town as most of the stores had been emptied in the first wave of panic shopping, and there was still no power to fire up either the cooling units in the stores or the diesel pumps for the transport trucks.

The number of people moving in or out had fizzled to almost nothing, but there were new and different visitors to the shack.

These folks came in old farm type trucks or less often on foot. They weren't passing through; they lived in the area and were yesterday's smug preppers and today's righteous looters. They'd stocked up and prepared for six months like their preparedness gurus had told them to. They had guns and ammo and canned goods and dry goods to last for half a year.

When it was pointed out to them from folks not 'in the know' like they were that the End of the World would most likely last longer than that and what would they do for food then?, they answered matter of factly with, "Well- we'll have the guns and ammo- when we run out of anything we'll *take* what we need".

When the solar storm hit, these groups went to ground like lightening-struck rabbits. And like ticks after winter, they started surfacing at the six month mark on the nosie- armed to the teeth and feeling justified in taking anything they needed...because they needed it and if you didn't care enough about your stuff to be ready, armed and willing to kill for it...oh, well.

Mostly they were bullies who made a lot of noise and took anything of value back to their lairs, bragging about the 'losers' they had taken food and supplies from.

The first group who came to the shack took everything that had been left for travelers, some of the furniture, and then 'just for fun' they shot out the windows.

The second group took the rest of the furniture, took an axe to the walls and took the time to scrawl apocalyptic bible verses on the walls in bold black lettering.

The third group used the shack as a place to drink, lined the empty cans on the windowsills and target practiced from the inside out; the bullets whizzing through the forest directly towards the hidden houses and their occupants.

"It's time." Athalie said quietly as the Shadows surveyed the shack one morning after it was again empty.

And everyone agreed.

Little Ray nudged an empty beer can with his foot and the slightest tendril of cigarette smoke wafted out the teardrop shaped opening and into the air.

Word around town was that one of the local idiots had dropped a still hot butt onto the floor of that cluttered, ravaged old wooden deer lease shack outside town.

Structure like that doesn't take long to burn down.

CHAPTER ELEVEN

The leaves rustled imperceptibly. There was no wind to speak of, and the air was heavy with heat.

Slowly but surely, the power grid inched back into working order. Factories were re-worked to use either manpower or to take advantage of the alternative energy sources that had been tentatively and reluctantly tapped...before.

One by tortuous one the huge transformers were replaced and set back in place. Electric wire was restrung and bit by bit the Americas turned on again.

The big cities came to life first, followed by the smaller towns in an ever wider ripple of awakening.

Contrarily, the closer the outlying areas came to being back to 'normal', the more frantic the isolationist groups seemed to get.

Those who had planned for years for the End of the World- stockpiling food and guns and ammo and toilet paper inside their bunkers and fortresses, spending thousands of dollars in ammunition target practicing at life sized zombies and training their children in military tactics couldn't believe they were being cheated...again.

Less than two decades previous, they'd made the same careful preparations for Y2K...and nothing happened. Not a blip. They were heartbroken.

But they'd held tight to their MRE's and their survival seeds and accumulated even more because they *knew* someday...

Someday there would be validation.

Someday was finally here. Every home they raided, every window broken and door bashed in, every family bullied while their meager valuables taken were sweet justice- *now* who was laughing? *Now* who was on top? They were.

Finally.

The Shadow group had been left in peace and overlooked because they were an almost complete non-presence and that was their entire goal- remain fed and sheltered and healthy while being so unobtrusive as to be completely invisible. Who was on top? They were.

That they were the only ones aware of it proved it.

In short order, everyone who wasn't part of the isolationists had been relieved of their possessions.

Everyone except...the other isolationists.

Because there were two groups in the area who 'went to ground' at the time of the event.

The above described group was heavy on guns and lived by the Lore of the Rugged Individualist- protect your own and screw everyone else- their kids learned the story of the Ants and the Grasshopper when they were tiny and no one wanted to be accused of being a Grasshopper.

The other group was also isolationists, but they had prepared for the End Times as described in the Good Book. They were heavy on bibles (and guns- in about equal measure) and lived by the predictions in Revelations- to prepare your families and ride it out until the Lord returned. They shunned sinners and heathens and were pretty isolated before the Solar Storm so it was easy for them to drop from sight when it happened.

They were also dismayed at the steady and seemingly unavoidable return to 'normalcy' because it meant that the Lord's return was not, in fact, imminent and they were not, in

fact, going to be riding to Glory on the Big Bus
to Heaven with all the other righteous servants.

Needless to say, both of these underground
communities were disillusioned, depressed,
pissed off and looking for someone to blame for
the ruination of all their dreams come true,
which was of course the end of the modern
world as everyone knew it.

The meltdown of the electric grid had meant
the end of an entire modern culture- no phones
or heat or air conditioning or gasoline.
Shortages of food and water and medications.
People without employment or transportation
or homes or assurance of their next meal.

Death and illness and wholesale despair of an
entire society.

It had been fleeting, but oh, so sweet.

And now it was over.

Damn it.

CHAPTER TWELVE

The leaves rustled imperceptibly. There was no wind to speak of, and the air was heavy with heat.

Shayla and Athalie were on a foraging hike and had gone farther than they had in the past. They were following the creek upstream, collecting Arrowhead tubers- a plentiful and year-round replacement for potatoes.

They waded the creek and marveled at the sparkling ripples created by little strider insects as well as the different plants and foliage that grew down in and along the creek bed; a whole different eco-system than just a dozen feet above them where Prickly Pear cactus nestled in a sea of pine needles.

At first they didn't even hear the voices, even though they were loud and strident.

It was no secret that the two isolationist groups resented each other- they had both raided the 'outsiders' periodically as they themselves ran out of supplies and it never failed to annoy them when the other group had beaten them to a target. They'd pout and cuss retreat back to their super-secret enclaves that weren't secret except in their own minds because everyone knew exactly where they were. They pretended not to know, though, because those rugged individualists were so unattractive when they sulked.

And now, with the world inconveniently threatening to fall back into place all around them, their nerves were worn completely thin and they were ready to lash out at an enemy...any enemy.

So they turned on each other.

Word around each of the compounds was that the other group had everything they needed. Everything. Not only that, they'd taken supplies from the outsiders that they didn't even need...just to keep each other from getting them.

Pre-emptive looting. Very un-ethical.

Patience wore thin, anger seethed and grew and spread like cancer, and it was only a matter of time.

Both groups felt acutely the need to assert their authority over the other one before the world shifted back on its axis and they were both relegated to irrelevance.

"All we want is for ya'll to give us what we were fixin' to rightfully take from the outsiders! Our people are hungry and we need that food! The

Lord told us that He would provide- it's evil for you to have taken what the Lord gave to us!"

The shouted reply dripped with sarcasm. "Sorry, dude! The Lord Giveth and WE tooketh away!"

Laughter rippled over the barricaded gate, sharp and sinister.

Shayla and Athalie were ankle-deep in the creek, the steep banks and dense foliage making them invisible to anyone above. Shayla looked around quickly and motioned Athalie into the shallow cave formed by a huge sweet gum tree's roots clawing their way out of the vertical bank, suspended in mid-air; reaching, reaching.

The creek ran quietly yet steadily, completely unconcerned about the drama on either side- one armed encampment being set upon by another and both 100% sure of their righteousness.

"I'm asking you nicely for the last time- do not interfere in the Lord's work!" shouted the man from the woods, and he was emboldened to move out into the open. He was tall and lean and silver-haired but not old or infirm. Looking up from the shelter of their hiding place, Shayla and Athalie could see the preacher's pristine white collar silhouetted against his jet black jacket.

"I'm warning you, Jedediah- go on back to ya'lls place and no one will get hurt."

Jedediah was unflappable, being on the Lord's team and all, and he strode to the top of the creek bank.

"Stop! This is your last warning to get off of our land and git on back home!"

"For Heaven's sake, Jacob- what are you going to do? Shoot me? We've known each other all our lives!" and Jedediah started to chuckle.

The gunshot from behind and off to the right of Jacob caught everyone off-guard, especially Jedediah, who dropped like a rock and was still- a small rivulet of scarlet puddling next to the snowy collar now scuffed with the red clay soil he lay on.

All eyes followed the invisible trail of death and at the end of it was a young man whose face was at first vindictively proud and angry, but as they watched the realization of what he'd done set in his expression changed from perplexed to confused to fearful before his head disappeared from view below the rim of the jagged rampart.

The gate to the enclosure flew open and Jacob ran out, horrified. He stared at the body across the creek for a split second; then seemed to notice for the first time the rest of the people who were with Jedediah, who had been frozen for an instant and who were now surrounding his body- now staring into his lifeless eyes, now up at the enclosure and straight through Jacob.

As if watching a movie, Jacob saw the distracted hatred in Jedediah's son's eyes, saw the gun raise up, heard the shot and then nothing. Ever again.

Shayla had clutched Athalie to her at the sound of the first shot and at the second one she instinctively covered her ears. There was no way this was going to end well.

Athalie's eyes were squeezed shut against the insanity around her and she was grateful that her mother had insisted that Olive stay home...just this once. When they had pushed into the shelter of the tree roots the small dark damp space filled with spiders and crawly things and heavens knew what else had frightened her- it seemed like a gnarly cage. Now she wished that the roots would close completely around them to keep them safe. Anything that was lurking in the tree roots was preferable to the madness up on the banks.

The death of a leader will cause one of two things to happen.

Sometimes with no one giving clear directions, the entire organization falls apart and the resulting splinters are ineffective and disburse without further trouble.

Or, there is an immediate and intense lust for revenge.

Two leaders lay fallen and two sets of followers were wild with desire for instant and final retribution.

One by one the people surrounding Jedediah's body fell, the cacophony of gunshots so intense it seemed violent enough to fell them without actual ammunition behind it.

It was still echoing through the forest as Shayla and Athalie peered upwards to see one man- one man rise up to a sitting position. There was a growing blackish-maroon stain oily and primal on the center of his shirt but he ignored it, grimaced and pulled back his arm.

His eyes were filled with fire that was not from Above, and the grenade arced gracefully and silently across the creek and disappeared behind the wall as gently and innocently as a feather.

"Oh, shit- hang on, Baby!" Shayla whispered and frantically covered Athalie's ears, pulling her as close as possible without hurting her. She turned where she sat, putting Athalie between her own body and the bank of the creek and braced herself.

The last thing she saw before the blast physically shoved them hard against the tree was the man who had thrown the grenade falling forward from the effort and not moving again.

EPILOGUE

Silence exploded around them, echoing in their ears with physical intensity and vibrating as though they'd been in the center of the world's worst thunderstorm.

Which, of course, they had been.
Metaphorically speaking.

"Are they gone, now?" the girl whispered timidly.

Her mother smiled warmly under weary eyes. "Yes, darlin'. That's the last of 'em". To no one but herself she added, "Poor bastards" under her breath.

She took her daughter's hand and they walked together away from the carnage and into the sunlight.

POSTSCRIPT

All characters in this story are fictitious. Any resemblance to anyone living or dead is purely coincidental.

The solar storm, however, is very real and will impersonally render society as we know it extremely inconvenient for at least a while.

For more information on solar storms, please see the very public FEMA document "Critical Communications During and After a Solar Superstorm". It's got lots of figures and a really cool timeline you can click through quickly and actually watch the shut-down of the grid.

Awesome

Sheri Dixon lives with her family in a log cabin in the pineywoods of East Texas.

While they endeavor to be the best homesteaders they can be given their physical and financial limitations, Sheri is quick to acknowledge that while she's pretty good with livestock, her yearly vegetable garden is always a crap shoot and mostly experimental.

To that end, she is busily learning what in the lush forests surrounding their home grows without help (also known as 'weeds') and is if not nutritious, at least not toxic.

Sheri recommends collecting books on wild edibles along with gardening and livestock manuals, as well as "Where There is No Doctor" and "Where There is No Dentist" as absolute musts for every home library.

Just in case.

Please visit Sheri at www.sheri-dixon.com

unimpressive   Sheri Dixon

unimpressive   Sheri Dixon

unimpressive   Sheri Dixon

unimpressive   Sheri Dixon